Moose
on the
Loose

By John and Ann Hassett

DOWN EAST BOOKS

8   10   12   14   15   13   11   9   7

Down East Books
P.O. Box 679
Camden, ME 04843
BOOK ORDERS: 1-800-685-7962

For Katie and Waldo

Deep in the forests of Maine, by a small blue pond, lived a moose named Max.

Max was a curious moose, and a curious moose asks lots of questions, like, "Why are my feet cold in the winter?" "Why do antlers look like tree branches?" and "Do you think there are moose on the moon?"

The other moose of the pond thought Max was foolish to ask such questions. "Eat your pond weeds and act like a moose!" was all they said.

"I do not like pond weeds," mumbled Max to himself, as he wondered what moon-moose might eat.

One day, as Max was busy thinking curious thoughts, a group of hikers appeared at the water's edge. The other moose lifted their mighty heads and looked. "Gurumph, only *people*," they grumbled and went back to eating. But Max had never seen "people" before, and he was very curious.

Max watched the people, and the people watched Max. He thought they were the most curious creatures he had ever seen. They made funny noises, and they stood on just two feet!

"Where did they come from?" Max wondered. "Are they here to eat the pond weeds, too?"

The other moose only answered, as they always did, "Eat your pond weeds, Max."

Max watched quietly as the people set out a picnic lunch. To his surprise, they ate things that were not pond weed, and they drank things that were not pond water.

"How very strange!" thought Max.

After a time, as suddenly as the hikers had appeared at the pond, they disappeared back into the forest. Max, who was now as curious as a curious moose could ever be, followed them into the woods.

But Max was not a good follower,
and he was soon hopelessly lost.

After much crashing and smashing through the brush and bracken, Max came upon a family of beavers working by a brook. "Perhaps these beavers have seen the people," thought Max. But when the beavers spotted Max, they dove to the bottom of the brook, for the beavers were rather small, and Max was rather large.

Max continued on, smashing and crashing his way through the forest, until he saw an owl sleeping in an old tree.

"Have you seen any people?" Max asked hopefully.

"Whoo?" said the sleepy owl.

"People," said Max.

"Whoo?" again replied the sleepy owl.

"PEOPLE!" Max yelled.

"Whoo?" the owl answered.

This might have gone on for a very long time if Chick the chickadee had not been flying by. "I know about people," said Chick, landing next to the owl, who had gone back to sleep. "There are many people in the town."

"Many people?" exclaimed Max. "In the town?"

"Of course," said Chick. "Why, there are as many people as there are pine cones in the forest. They live in houses. I fly there sometimes, and they feed me seeds." Chick knew a lot and was very brave.

Max became more and more curious at the thought of seeing *many* people, so Chick agreed to show the curious moose how to find the town. He led Max to the forest edge. "This is the highway," said Chick. "It's a path the people travel on, and it leads to the people's town."

Max saw many brightly colored objects zipping past. "Those are cars," explained Chick. "The people sit inside them and go up and back, up and back, all day long and into the night."

"How very strange," thought Max. "I will follow this people-path and find where the people live."

"Bring me back some seeds if you can, Moose," said Chick as he flew off. He had an appointment to see a new hole in a hollow tree.

Max trotted happily down the road. *Cloppity, cloppity, clop,* his hooves sounded on the hard pavement. The cars whizzed wildly around him like bees. Max hoped a car might stop so he could say hello, but none did. They just zoomed past.

On and on and on Max walked until finally he saw a house, then another house, then another, and many more houses up ahead.

"This must be where the people live," said Max as he cheerfully trotted into a back yard.

"Hello!" he said, poking his head into an open window. But no one was home except a cat and a parakeet, so he ate a plant that was sitting on the windowsill and hurried on.

Max went from house to house. He jumped fences, crashed through hedges, and got tangled in clotheslines.

Max crossed streets without even looking. "BEEP, BEEP! HONK, HONK!" cars tooted. He had seen many people by now. Some people made loud noises, some ran away, and some just quietly stared. Max just trotted on happily.

Max visited a gas station and tried to get into a car, as the people did, but he didn't fit. Then he went up the street and stood in a

swimming pool, which he liked very much. ("No pond weeds here!" he said.) He wandered down to the railroad tracks and watched the trains. *Wooo-oooo* they whistled, louder than the loudest moose in the forest. "How wonderful," the curious moose sighed.

Wherever Max went, people could not believe their eyes. A moose? On the loose? In the middle of town? Word spread quickly.

All that day and into the evening, reports of Max's travels came over the radio, for Max was far too excited to sleep that night.

"The moose has just been seen at the mill."

"The moose just went by the airport."

"The moose has just been seen at the drive-in."

The next day, things were very busy at the police station. "There's a moose drinking out of my birdbath!" someone reported.

"He took a nap on my porch," another said. "And now he's at the window, watching TV!"

It seemed that Max was everywhere. "HONK, HONK! BEEP, BEEP!" on South Street. "HONK, HONK! BEEP, BEEP!" as he went up Penobscot, down Broadway, then over to State Street.

Max was happily trotting by a tall building when he saw that the doors were open. As a curious moose will do, especially this curious moose, he went inside. He looked around and saw a large stairway. Up the stairs he began to climb. "I'll climb up this mountain," said Max happily. Up and up and up he went until he reached the roof.

"I will be able to see everything from up here,"
thought Max as he strolled to the edge. But as he
looked down, he felt a little dizzy. His legs got wobbly,
and his stomach did loops inside. Max didn't know it,
but he was afraid of heights. With a loud *plunk!* and a
plop! Max fainted.

The news traveled fast. "Hurry, hurry!" a boy shouted. "The moose has fainted atop the tallest building in town!"

"Quickly, quickly!" someone's grandmother added.

"This way to see the moose!" people yelled. It was not long before a huge crowd had gathered below.

When Max finally woke up, he found he could not get up. He could not go down. He could not move at all. Hours passed with poor Max stuck on top of the tallest building in town.

"Oh Chick," said Max, "I'm afraid the town is no place to visit if you cannot fly. But I am about to eat some delicious pond weeds. Will you join me for lunch?"

And Chick did.

Max was very frightened, and he was hungry, too.
For the first time, he missed his little pond and the
other moose in the forest.

"Ooooo," Max began to moan. "Ooooo," echoed
from the rooftop and was heard for miles.

Just then, something appeared high in the sky over Max. It was big, it was loud, and it was coming closer.

"Ooooo," moaned poor Max, more frightened than ever.

But the crowd below shouted, "Hurray!" They knew it was a helicopter sent to rescue Max.

The helicopter hovered over the building. A man inside lowered a rope, and another man tied it around the woozy moose.

"Ooooo," Max groaned as the helicopter lifted him off the building and up into the sky.

"Don't look down, you silly moose!" the people shouted from below. Max shut his eyes and kept them closed tight.

Over houses, highways, and hilltops soared the helicopter, with Max dangling below.

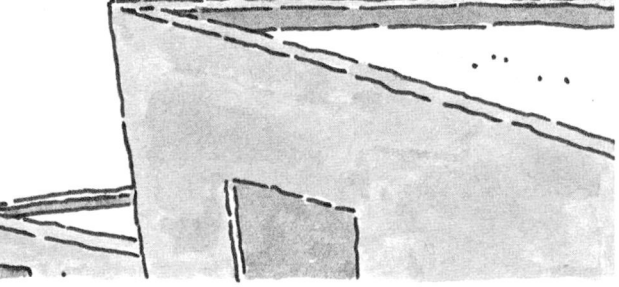

On and on and on they flew, over farms, fields, and forests, until at last the helicopter hovered over one spot.

Just then, Chick the chickadee fluttered up next to Max and landed on one of his antlers. "Hello again, Moose. I see you forgot my seeds."

Max opened his eyes and looked down. Below he saw, small and blue, his little pond and the other moose happily eating pond weeds.